The Children of
TOPAZ

The Children of
TOPAZ

The Story of a Japanese-American Internment Camp

Based on a Classroom Diary

by Michael O. Tunnell
and George W. Chilcoat

Holiday House/New York

The pages of "Our Daily Diary," photographed by M. O. Tunnell, were reproduced with the permission of the Utah State Historical Society, which also gave permission to reproduce all other photographs in this book, except those noted below and those appearing on pages 17, 22, 66 (right), 68, 69 and 70.

The class picture on the jacket and on page 66 is reprinted by permission of Saburo Hori.

The photograph of four women in front of Sather Gate, University of California at Berkeley, on page 42 is reproduced with the permission of Takako Endo.

The poem on page 12, "Plate in Hand" by Yukari, is reprinted by permission of University of Washington Press, Seattle, Washington.

Library of Congress Cataloging-in-Publication Data
Tunnell, Michael O.
The children of Topaz : the story of a Japanese-American
internment camp : based on a classroom diary / by Michael O. Tunnell
and George W. Chilcoat. — 1st ed.
p.   cm.
Includes bibliographical references.
Summary: The diary of a third-grade class of Japanese-American
children being held with their families in an internment camp during
World War II.
ISBN 0-8234-1239-3
1. Japanese Americans—Evacuation and relocation, 1942–1945—
Juvenile literature.   2. World War, 1939–1945—Children—United
States—Juvenile literature.   3. Central Utah Relocation Center—
Juvenile literature.   [1. Japanese Americans—Evacuation and
relocation, 1942–1945.   2. World War, 1939–1945—Children.
3. Central Utah Relocation Center.]   I. Chilcoat, George W.
II. Title.
D769.8.A6T86   1996   95–49360   CIP   AC
940.53′1779245—dc20

To Lillian "Anne" Yamauchi Hori and her 1943 class
of third-grade students at Topaz, Utah.

INTRODUCTION

"*Tora! Tora! Tora!*" Shortly before 8:00 A.M. on December 7, 1941, these code words streaked across the airwaves from the dive-bomber of Commander Mitsuo Fuchida. They were a signal to the high command of the Japanese Imperial Navy that Japanese aircraft had just attacked the American naval base at Pearl Harbor, Hawaii. Up until then, Japan and the United States had not been at war, although World War II was raging on much of the planet. The Japanese air raid caught the U.S. Navy by surprise. On that sleepy Sunday morning, sailors and airmen could hardly man their battle stations before the Japanese dive-bombers destroyed or crippled almost all the ships and airplanes at Pearl Harbor and killed or wounded about 3,500 people. When the attack was over, a large part of the U.S. Naval Fleet in the Pacific Ocean was lost.

The United States immediately declared war on Japan. This was a nightmare for Americans, who had been hoping to stay out of World War II. And to make things worse, war with Japan automatically meant war with Hitler's Germany, because these two hostile nations, along with Italy, were allies. When Pearl Harbor was attacked, Germany already had been at war with the rest of Europe for more than two years. Now, American soldiers would be fighting and dying in both the South Pacific and Europe.

At home in the United States, people were angry and afraid. The war in Europe had seemed far away, and now it had come to America's doorstep. If the Japanese had attacked Americans in Hawaii, what would keep them from dive-bombing Los Angeles or Seattle? Fiery patriotic propaganda against Japan filled newspapers and radio broadcasts, and many Americans were overcome by an irrational hatred of anything Japanese—including fellow Americans who wore Japanese faces.

In 1941, there were about 125,000 people of Japanese ancestry, called

Reaction to the bombing of Pearl Harbor was swift and hostile. Many businesses refused to serve Japanese Americans.

Nikkei (*Neek-kay*), living in the United States, not including the territory of Hawaii. Most of them lived on the West Coast and, like the rest of the country's immigrant population, were usually hardworking, patriotic Americans. The problem was that because of their Japanese ancestry, they looked like the enemy. Of course, Germans and Italians were U.S. enemies, too, but German and Italian Americans resembled English and French Americans. Even though two-thirds of the Nikkei in the United States were born here and were American citizens, they suddenly became aliens and enemies in the eyes of many other Americans because of their distinctive skin color and features. One newspaper columnist even advised his readers to learn the differences among the Koreans, Chinese, and Japanese so that they could "be sure of nationality" before they were "rude to anybody."

People on the West Coast of the United States reacted vi ' ⁒ly to the Nikkei living there. But even well before Pearl Harb   oastal residents resented them. In fact, the United States governm ı⁹ always had denied citizenship to first-generation Japanese immigrants, called the Issei (*Ees-say*). The Naturalization Act of 1790 limited the granting of U.S. citizenship to "free white person[s]," and although later amendments provided citizenship rights for Africans and even for other Asians, the Issei continued to be denied. In the Pacific states, they were not even allowed to own land or marry outside their race—in a country established by immigrants, no less! It was not uncommon to see billboards during the 1920s, 1930s, and early 1940s on the West Coast that read "Japs, don't let the sun shine on you here. Keep moving," or "Japs keep moving. This is a white man's neighborhood." Much of this racism was kindled when the Issei first arrived on the West Coast and, against all odds, became successful farmers. Because they were refused most other jobs and could not own their own land, the Issei took rocky, unwanted plots of rented land and converted them into thriving farms. By 1941, these farms were producing over one-third of the truck crops (vegetables) in California. Other farmers were jealous. Also, because the Issei were shunned by most Americans, they created their own society within a society in order to feel safe and to have friends. This made them seem even more remote and strange.

The children of the Issei, called the Nisei (*Nee-say*), could not be denied U.S. citizenship because they were born on American soil. Unlike their parents, they tried to blend into American society as much as possible, sometimes even feeling ashamed of their "Japaneseness." Still, opportunities were not equal for the Nisei. One Nisei student recalled a high-school teacher discouraging him from selecting many of the majors that his white friends were pursuing in college. "Then the teacher told me outright in a very nice way that there was not much of a chance for an Oriental to get a job in these fields. . . . I began to see that they took us a little differently and we were not quite American in their eyes in spite of things they taught us in the classes about equality and so forth." Young Nisei engineering graduates would end up as gardeners or store clerks because no one would hire them. People joked that a creatively stacked fruit display meant the Japanese clerk was an engineer. Despite the fact that Japanese-American students were consistently among the highest achievers in school, discrimination persisted.

Therefore, when Pearl Harbor was attacked, people who already were prejudiced against the Japanese Americans suddenly had a reason to justify all their old hatreds. Restaurants and stores refused service to the Nikkei. More nasty and threatening signs appeared in shop windows and on billboards. Although the Nikkei as a group were extremely patriotic Americans, nothing they did seemed to convince other Americans of their loyalty.

[3]

This sign on a Japanese-American grocery store seems to cry out, "Please believe me!"

Japanese Americans were as stunned by the attack on Pearl Harbor as the rest of the country. Many of the Nisei were furious. *"They* are attacking *us!"* yelled a Nisei high-school student. The Japanese American Citizen's League (JACL), an organization that battled discrimination by encouraging outspoken patriotism among its members, immediately sent a telegram to President Franklin Delano Roosevelt. It boldly stated: "We are ready and prepared to expend every effort to repel this invasion together with our fellow Americans." In days to come, the JACL even organized war bond and Red Cross drives and worked with the FBI to locate possible enemies within the Japanese-American population.

The Issei were fearful and ashamed. Not only did they have the faces of the enemy, but they were also still citizens of Japan. Some of the elders tried desperately to cut ties with their Japanese heritage by burying mementos such as samurai swords and traditional Japanese clothing. They cleansed their homes of Japanese language magazines and books, Buddhist shrines (evidence of a religion strange to the Western world), and even family photographs of relatives in Japan.

But neither the Nisei's patriotic words and actions nor the Issei's efforts to appear more Americanized seemed to help. Destructive, unthinking reactions to Pearl Harbor erupted from the worst person-

Vandals strike out against the Nikkei by breaking headstones on Japanese-American graves.

alities. In Washington, D.C., an unidentified "patriot" chopped down several Japanese cherry trees in a senseless act of anger. Japanese cemeteries were vandalized, as were the homes of Japanese Americans. Nikkei farms were terrorized, and, in a few cases, anti-Japanese fanatics shot and killed innocent people.

Even the more civilized elements of American society seemed infected by the war hysteria. Newspapers fanned the fire by continuing to print shocking and unfounded stories about Japanese Americans and using the same term for the Nikkei as was being used for the enemy—"Japs." Rumors about spies raced through communities like wildfire: the "Japs" in Hawaii had cut arrows into their crops that guided the attack force to Pearl Harbor; the "Japs" in California were in contact with Japanese submarines and were prepared to sabotage airports, power plants, or other military targets. Although some of these rumors are still believed today, there was never a single confirmed case of Japanese-American spying or sabotage. In fact, when President Franklin Roosevelt asked for a careful survey of Japanese Americans, it was reported that they possessed "a remarkable, even extraordinary degree of loyalty."

The U.S. government turned out to be as suspicious and mistrusting as any of the groups that were angrily pointing their fingers at the

Nikkei. Within hours of the attack on Pearl Harbor, FBI agents broke into and searched the homes of respected members of the Japanese-American community—without search warrants. Then, over 1,300 men, mostly Issei, were arrested and taken from their families without any explanation. Yoshiko Uchida remembered the terrible worry: "All that day and for three days that followed, we had no knowledge of what had happened to my father." Probably for no other reason but their "Japaneseness," the arrested men were suspected of being disloyal. They were asked stupid questions, such as "If you had a gun in your hand, at whom would you shoot, the Americans or the Japanese?" (Most answered that they'd shoot "straight up.") In the end, 336, including Yoshiko's father, were sent to internment camps in Montana or South Dakota.

The Constitution of the United States guarantees the right to privacy, protecting people from having the police search their homes without authorization from the courts. It also guarantees the right to due process. "Due process" means that fair legal procedures must be followed before a person can be convicted of a crime. These basic rights, so fundamental to what the United States of America stands for, were simply cast aside for these Japanese-American men because they were deemed "enemy aliens." They were sent to internment camps without a fair trial, and, in the following weeks, nearly all of the Nikkei on the West Coast suffered a similar fate.

The people and the government seemed to demand that the Japanese Americans be treated as a threat to U.S. security. On February 19, 1942, President Roosevelt signed Executive Order 9066, giving the army the power to establish military zones in the United States "from which any or all persons may be excluded as deemed necessary." Although the order didn't specifically mention the Japanese Americans, the army immediately labeled the West Coast as such an area and then imposed an 8:00 P.M. curfew and a five-mile travel limit on all the Nikkei. The Japanese-American community was required to turn in any shortwave radios, cameras, binoculars, and guns—items handy to spies. Everyone knew that soon the Japanese Americans would be forced to leave their homes; the government would move them to special camps far from the coast. By the middle of March, the removal of "enemy aliens" began. Though the parents of baseball hero Joe DiMaggio were technically "enemy aliens"—they were Italian citizens living in San Francisco—no one dreamed of forcing them from their home. Yet the Nisei, who were United States citizens, were relocated.

This headline in the *San Francisco Examiner* fueled hatred for the Nikkei by using the negative term "Japs."

Lieutenant General John L. DeWitt was in charge of moving people of Japanese ancestry away from strategic locations on the West Coast (airports, dams, power plants, the ocean front). He justified his actions by saying: "It makes no difference whether the Japanese is theoretically a citizen. He is still Japanese. Giving him a scrap of paper doesn't change him." DeWitt kept enlarging the areas from which he wanted enemy aliens removed until he achieved his goal: the relocation of virtually all the Nikkei living in California, Oregon, and Washington.

Comments by other well-known or powerful people only helped public opinion swing further against the Nikkei. Newspaper columnist Henry McLemore, who wrote for the influential Hearst publishing dynasty, was bold enough to say: "I am for immediate removal of every Japanese on the West Coast to a point deep in the interior. Herd 'em up, pack 'em off and give 'em the inside room in the badlands. Let 'em be pinched, hurt, hungry, and dead against it. . . . Personally, I hate the Japanese. And that goes for all of them." A farm leader in California openly admitted wanting to get rid of the Japanese for selfish reasons. "If all the Japs were removed tomorrow, we'd never miss them in two weeks, because the white farmers can take over and produce everything the Jap grows. And we don't want them back when the war ends either." It is not surprising that a Gallup opinion poll in early 1942 showed that while hatred for Germany was centered on evil leaders like Adolf Hitler, hatred for Japan was centered on an entire race of people.

Although the U.S. government permitted the Nikkei to voluntarily relocate to parts of the country farther inland, few had places to go or could afford to move so far away. Many of the five thousand who did move had a hard time. Some were met at the California-Nevada border by men with guns who turned them away. Even the governor of Kansas had the highway patrol keep Japanese-American travelers from entering his state.

Beginning February 25, 1942, the West Coast Nikkei began receiving orders from the U.S. Army to abandon their homes and move to the relocation camps. Usually they had to be ready to leave within ten days—ten days to store or sell their belongings, to sell or find someone to manage their businesses, to put all their affairs in order, and to pack only as much as they could carry. "How can we clear out in ten days a house we've lived in for fifteen years?" asked Iku Uchida, whose orders came on April 21. It was a question that was asked over and over by many families. Although the government stored the belongings of the Nikkei who had no other options, it was "at the sole risk of the owner." Many never saw their things again.

And who had to go? Anyone with a Japanese ancestor, even if the relationship was so remote that the individual had neither Japanese features nor ties to the Japanese community. And part-Japanese families—those with a white husband or wife—were not spared. Either they were separated or the white partner chose to go along with his or her spouse. Mary Kimura, a Portuguese immigrant, accompanied her half-Japanese son to the Topaz Relocation Center.

Nikkei families were registered and given a number. "From that day on," said Yoshiko Uchida, "we became Family Number 13453." Her family was given baggage and name tags with their number printed on them. They attached these labels to themselves and their possessions on E-Day (Evacuation Day). E-Day for the Uchidas, who lived in Berkeley, California, was May 1, 1942. They, like other families and single men and women, gathered at the First Congregational Church, toting as many of their belongings as they could carry. They were loaded into buses and taken to the Tanforan Assembly Center in San Bruno, California. Tanforan was one of several temporary camps where the Nikkei were held until the more permanent and remote relocation centers were constructed.

Taking only a few suitcases, the Japanese Americans left most of their lives behind—their friends, pets, and dreams for the future. One young Nisei put it this way: "You never thought such a thing could

[8]

happen to you, but it has. And you feel all tangled up inside because you do not quite see the logic of having to surrender freedom in a country that you sincerely feel is fighting for freedom."

It was an unhappy, lonely time. "Before we went my sister and I went into every room of our house and the garden and waved them good-bye," said another Nisei child. For many children, the most traumatic experience was leaving behind their family dogs and cats, since animals were not allowed to go with them.

In later years, Amy Iwasaki Mass realized that taking her pet to be left at a neighbor's was so disturbing that she had repressed the memory. She finally remembered years later when her older sister began talking about how difficult this event had been for Amy.

Here is what another child wrote about leaving his collie (original spelling and punctuation left intact):

> He knew something was wrong. . . . He suspected because we were carrying our suitcases with us. When we were going down our garden . . . he followed us. I told him to go home he just sat and howled and cryed. My cousin and I got mad at him but we love him almost as if he were a human being. . . . When we drove away from the front of the house he was sitting inside the fence looking out.

The evacuation was perhaps even more difficult for adults. World War I veteran Hideo Murata could not believe what was happening. Instead of reporting to be evacuated, he paid in advance for a hotel room and then killed himself. In his hand he clutched the Certificate of Honorary Citizenship presented to him on July 4, 1941, by Monterey County, California—a "testimony of heartfelt gratitude, of honor and respect for your loyal and splendid service to the country."

The U.S. Army was in charge of the assembly centers, which were enclosed in barbed wire and guarded like prisoner-of-war camps. Tanforan Assembly Center was a hastily converted racetrack that housed eight thousand Japanese Americans. Many of the dwellings were converted horse stalls, although black tar-papered shacks had been quickly built. The Uchidas found themselves in a 10-by-20-foot stall with a layer of linoleum laid over manure-covered boards and a few army cots on which to sleep. Dirty and smelling of horses, this unfurnished "apartment" was their home for the next four-and-a-half months. Suddenly, families who were used to preparing meals and sitting together around a dining room table had to stand in long mess

A Japanese-American veteran of World War I protests relocation.

Horse-stall apartments at Tanforan Assembly Center.

hall lines to eat unappetizing food. There was little privacy as people were jammed into barracks with thin walls and forced to use community latrines that had no doors on the stalls. "I felt degraded, humiliated, and overwhelmed with longing for home," said Yoshiko Uchida. "And I saw the unutterable sadness on my mother's face."

The assembly centers prepared their inhabitants for what in many cases were even worse conditions in the relocation camps. But the uncomfortable living arrangements were not nearly as upsetting as the armed guards and the barbed-wire fences that surrounded Tanforan. The Nikkei were no longer free. Here a young child writes about life in the shadows of Tanforan's guard towers.

> We have roll call about 6:30 every day.
> I'm at the rec hall every day before roll call we are playing Basket ball or swinging on the bars.
> When the siren ring I get so scared that I sometime scream some people gets scared of me instead of the siren we run home as fast as I could then we wait about 5 minutes then the inspectore come to check that we are all home. . . .
> After the camp roll call finish the siren rings again. . . . I hate roll call because it scares you to much.

Within the confines of the assembly centers, the Japanese Americans tried to create a community. They organized schools, camp newspapers, sports programs, and talent shows. But the air of uncertainty and the nature of camp life began to strain family relationships. This

The nursery school at Tanforan that was started by Keiko and Yoshiko Uchida. Years later, Yoshiko wrote several books about her relocation experiences, including *Journey to Topaz.*

poem by Iku Uchida (who wrote under the name Yukari) expresses the sadness and yet the strength of the evacuees:

Plate in hand,
I stand in line,
Losing my resolve
To hide my tears.

I see my mother
In the aged woman
    who comes,
And I yield to her
My place in line.

Four months have passed,
And at last I learn
To call this horse stall
My family's home.

Yukari

In the fall of 1942, the assembly centers were emptied, and over 110,000 people of Japanese ancestry were loaded onto trains and sent to war relocation centers in Poston and Gila, Arizona; Manzanar and Tule Lake, California; Rohwer and Jerome, Arkansas; Heart Mountain, Wyoming; Minidoka, Idaho; Granada, Colorado; and Topaz, Utah. These centers were administered by the War Relocation Authority (WRA) rather than by the army. The first director of the WRA, Milton Eisenhower, wanted to move the Japanese Americans into communities around the country. But he was met by such fierce opposition from most states (governors in the western states would only accept the Nikkei under armed guard) that he resorted instead to creating relocation camps. These were not much different from the assembly centers. Later, Eisenhower wrote in a letter, "I feel most deeply that when this war is over and we consider calmly this unprecedented migration of 120,000 people, we as Americans are going to regret the unavoidable injustices that may have been done."

The people living in Tanforan Assembly Center were sent to Topaz—a three-day trip in an old, rickety train from San Bruno, California, to Delta, Utah. When the unwilling passengers arrived in Delta, they were loaded onto buses and taken seventeen miles out into the Sevier Desert. It was there, in the harsh, windblown desert, that many Japanese-American children spent much of their childhood. They

Guarded as though they were dangerous war criminals, Japanese-American families arrive by train in Delta, Utah.

played, attended school, became Cub Scouts and Brownies, and celebrated holidays mostly within the one square mile of barbed wire, dust, and tar-paper barracks officially called the Central Utah Relocation Center.

In spite of the desolate and unhappy circumstances in which these children found themselves, they managed to find wonder and pleasure in their desert world. Good teachers and strong parents helped smooth away at least some of the trouble for them. One such teacher was Lillian "Anne" Yamauchi Hori, whose third-grade class at Topaz's Mountain View School kept a diary. More than fifty years later, its

After a dusty bus ride from Delta, the new residents of Topaz Relocation Center were processed at this induction center.

words and drawings speak to us about the injustice experienced by the children of Topaz.

"Our Class Diary" begins on March 8, 1943. March 8 was well into the regular school year, but because the school barracks were not ready when the children arrived in Topaz, Mountain View School got a late start. That year, classes ran through the summer so that children could make up for the lost time.

In the camp elementary schools, the teachers and students held informal talks each morning. Teachers hoped this time of sharing thoughts and ideas would help the children broaden their interests and learn to express their feelings about their surroundings. Informal discussions would also give the students an opportunity to build their vocabulary, which in turn would help them in speaking, reading, and writing.

Probably the morning talks generated much of what is found in the diary kept by Miss Yamauchi's class. Miss Yamauchi did the writing, recording what her third graders thought important. Then the children took turns illustrating each page. Twenty of the seventy-three diary pages appear in this book.

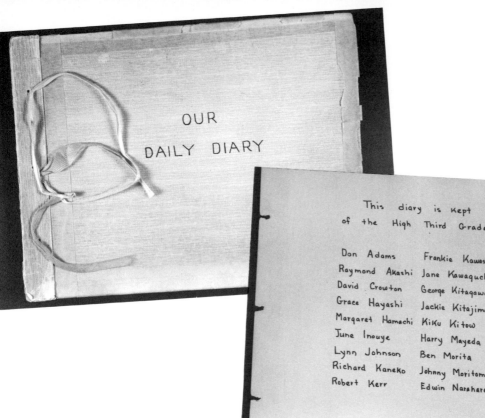

OUR
DAILY DIARY

This diary is kept by the members of the High Third Grade. Their names are:

Don Adams	Frankie Kawasaki	Shizuko Nishitani
Raymond Akashi	Jane Kawaguchi	Makoto Oda
David Crowton	George Kitagawa	Betty Sugiyama
Grace Hayashi	Jackie Kitajima	Robert Suzuki
Margaret Hamachi	Kiku Kitow	Kei Takemoto
June Inouye	Harry Mayeda	Roy Takeuchi
Lynn Johnson	Ben Morita	Kimiko Tsutsui
Richard Kaneko	Johnny Moritomo	Bobby Hirano
Robert Kerr	Edwin Narahara	Mae Yanagi

March 8, 1943

On March 7, Don went to the gravel pit and found some Topaz.

Miss Robertson told us today that we must be careful about touching jackrabbits because they have a disease. She told us also about a badger at Block 42. We shall go see it very soon.

The illustration for March 8 tells a lot about the children's surroundings. Although Topaz was dubbed "The Jewel of the Desert," the environment was, in Yoshiko Uchida's words, "as bleak as bleached bones." And bleached bones are exactly what this young artist drew— the skull and leg bone of a cow in the foreground of the picture. The dust devil or whirlwind in the upper left is another example of the dry, dusty climate. Trees couldn't survive; only a wiry, gray shrub called greasewood.

March 8, 1943.

On March 7, Don went to the gravel pit and found some Topaz.

Miss Robertson told us today that we must be careful about touching jack-rabbits because they have a disease. She told us also about a badger at Block 42. We shall go see it very soon.

The topaz that Don found in the gravel pit is a semiprecious stone, sometimes called a yellow sapphire. Internees (people confined against their will) often found pieces of topaz. Of course, this gives a double meaning to "The Jewel of the Desert." Was it the camp or the mineral?

The diary mentions Block 42, which gives us a hint about the layout of Topaz City. Topaz had 42 blocks of barracks. Each residential block contained 12 barracks and about 250 people, and was arranged around a mess hall, latrine-washrooms, and a laundry. The barracks were 120 feet long and 20 feet wide. They were divided into six rooms of varying sizes—a four-person room was 20 by 20 feet. An address in Topaz would read like this: Block 7, Barrack 2, Apt. C (or 7-2-C), Topaz, Utah.

Some of the blocks were used for schools and administration buildings. The two elementary schools, Mountain View and Desert View, were in Blocks 8 and 41 respectively. But thirty-four of the blocks were residential. This one-square-mile camp soon had a population of over eight thousand—the fifth largest city in Utah!

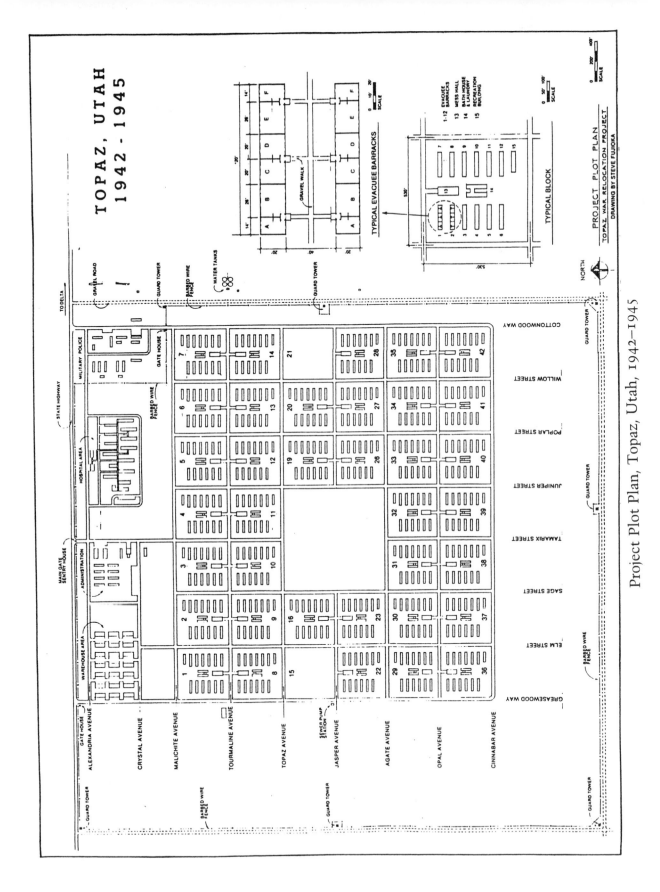

Project Plot Plan, Topaz, Utah, 1942–1945

March 11, 1943.

Yesterday we started to join the American Junior Red Cross.

Please remember to put 10% of your pay into war bonds and stamps. We should not kill spiders because Uncle Sam needs them for the war.

Lynn will get a new refrigerator today.

Blocks 3, 16, 22, 23 had no running water this morning because the water pipe broke at the high school grounds. The people in these blocks went to other places to wash their faces and brush their teeth.

March 11, 1943

Yesterday we started to join the American Junior Red Cross.

Please remember to put 10% of your pay into war bonds and stamps. We should not kill spiders because Uncle Sam needs them for the war.

Lynn will get a new refrigerator today.

Blocks 3, 16, 22, 23 had no running water this morning because the water pipe broke at the high school ground. The people in these blocks went to other places to wash their faces and brush their teeth.

Eleanor Gerard Sekerak, a white teacher at Topaz High School, noted that the core philosophy of the camp schools was to teach the democratic way of life. "As I faced my first day I wondered how I could teach American government and democratic principles while we sat in classrooms behind barbed wire!" She remembered a lump rising in her throat at the phrase, "liberty and justice for all." But Miss Yamauchi, a Nikkei teacher, apparently encouraged her students to be good Americans. They joined the American Red Cross, which sent supplies and other aid to American soldiers. In fact, "Please remember to put 10% of your pay into war bonds and stamps" almost sounds like a patriotic poster. Even though the internees were paid only a few dollars a month for the jobs they did around the camp, and despite their obvious loss of freedom, they still were willing to support the American war effort.

Part of supporting the war effort included being kind to spiders. Spiderwebs will not stretch or fray and were perfect for making the crosshairs in bombsights. Bombers, the most destructive American warplanes, used a sighting device with crossed lines like a rifle scope to aim the bombs dropped on German and Japanese targets.

The diary also mentions Lynn's new refrigerator. However, there wasn't adequate electricity in the barracks apartments of the Nikkei to operate such a convenience. One wire and one bulb hung in the middle of each room. The apartment didn't even have running water, which existed only in the latrines and laundries. In fact, the water system at Topaz caused continual problems. Blocks were often with-

Nisei children attending school in a barbed-wire enclosure are still willing to say "The Pledge of Allegiance." The child in the center is Mary Ann Yahiro, who lost both her home and her mother because of relocation. Her mother was moved to another camp where she died.

out water because the original water pipes were cheap and thin and the alkaline soil caused them to corrode and leak. Disputes over repairing the water system were ongoing between the residents and the administration of Topaz.

For the Japanese Americans, the camps offered few luxuries and few alternatives. The internees of Topaz formed a classless society where doctors and ditchdiggers found themselves on the same rung of the social ladder. In the camps, the Nikkei had no automobiles or fancy clothes. There were no prestigious stores or good restaurants. All former economic classes lined up together for movies that cost ten cents.

Obviously, Lynn Johnson did not live in a Nikkei apartment. He was the child of a white camp employee. White families had half a barrack—the same space occupied by three Japanese-American families—which was carpeted, furnished, and had a fully equipped kitchen.

White camp employees had the choice of sending their children to the schools in Topaz or letting them go to the public schools in Delta. Whites who understood and appreciated the Japanese-Americans knew that the Nisei students were hardworking. They wanted that kind of disciplined educational environment for their own children. So, students like Lynn attended school in Topaz.

March 19, 1943

We all delivered our letters to Miss Yamauchi because she will be married tomorrow.
Edwin played a joke on Miss Yamauchi.
It was Bobby's birthday yesterday. He is 9 years old.
Makoto made a kite that flew very high.
Lynn's father made him a kite.
Don's little brother has pneumonia.

Within the barbed-wire enclosure and under the barrels of rifles, the children of Topaz celebrated birthdays and giggled over the upcoming marriage of their teacher. Kite-making and flying were common pastimes for both children and adults, although on occasion kites would

March 19, 1943.

We all delivered our letters to Miss Yamauchi because she will be married tomorrow.

Edwin played a joke on Miss Yamauchi. It was Bobby's birthday yesterday. He is 9 years old.

Makoto made a kite that flew very high.

Lynn's father made him a kite.

Don's little brother has pneumonia.

fall and get tangled in the barbed wire. In the diary entry for March 19, the children drew kites flying over the open spaces of the camp. You can see the barbed-wire fence and guard tower in the background and the mountains on the horizon. Edwin Narahara, the boy mentioned in the diary who played a joke on Miss Yamauchi, remembered years later that he and many of his nine-year-old classmates didn't fully realize what had happened to them. In fact, Edwin thought Topaz was "like going on a camp-out!"

The photograph of the camp doesn't show guard towers as does the drawing. But make no mistake, this was a camp under armed guard—3 to 5 officers and 85 to 150 men were stationed at Topaz. The credentials of everyone entering and leaving the camp were checked. Guard towers located every quarter of a mile were manned with detachments of armed soldiers and were equipped with searchlights used to scout for possible nighttime escapees.

Saburo Hori, Miss Yamauchi's fiancé, and other Japanese-American engineers were put to work surveying and erecting the barbed-wire fence that was to enclose them. The Nikkei were told that one reason for relocating them away from the West Coast was for their own

[21]

A typical block of barracks at Topaz.

Miss Yamauchi and her new husband, Saburo Hori. Saburo was an engineer and was working on a graduate degree at the University of California at Berkeley when Pearl Harbor was attacked. *Saburo Hori*

protection. But internee Dave Tatsuno observed that "the machine guns and army rifles were turned not out, but inward."

Sickness was a problem, in part because of the living conditions. Roger Walker, a young sailor in the U.S. Navy who returned home to Delta, worked at the camp during its last year (1945). He felt the barracks did not provide proper shelter. "The sheeting had cracks at least a quarter of an inch between each board. . . . No insulation whatsoever . . . It was really difficult to see how they survived." Edwin Narahara remembered collecting milkweed pods to stuff in open spaces as insulation.

Carpenters finally installed Sheetrock in the barracks. Until then, dust and cold readily entered through large gaps in the walls.

Winter, of course, was the worst time. "Take warm clothes," advised the War Relocation Authority. "Utah winters are cold at 4,700 feet." New arrivals were issued two blankets apiece—insufficient for the cold nights. The emotional stress of being uprooted and moved to the desert also seemed to cause more illnesses—both physical and mental—than normally would be expected.

[23]

March 29, 1943

On March 28th, there was a fire at Block 22 at 11:30 P.M. It was on the roof of the laundry room. The fire was caused by sparks from the chimney. Don saw another fire on the way to Delta.

Today Miss Yamauchi came back to school. We voted for the name we liked best. Miss Yamauchi had twelve votes and Mrs. Hori had ten. We shall call her Miss Yamauchi, just like before.

Raymond and the Boy Scouts went for a hike yesterday. They used a neckerchief to signal to each other.

Fire was a constant threat at Topaz. Because of the tar-paper-and-wood construction, the barracks were firetraps. Potbellied stoves that burned coal and wood belched sparks that could easily ignite tarred roofs and tar-papered walls.

Another danger at Topaz was the dust storm. Upon arrival in Utah, one young Nisei wondered why a Japanese-American boy who came to meet the train had such white shoes. "I thought maybe he was working in a cement factory." But when the traveler got off the bus, he discovered that dust "just like cement powder" immediately whitened his shoes, too. Lying undisturbed on the ground, the dust was merely irritating when stirred by your feet. And for months, when the barracks were without the inner Sheetrock walls, gentle breezes filled the rooms with a thick layer of the stuff. But when the wild desert winds kicked up, the dust became a killer.

Yoshiko Uchida tells of a baptism by dust shortly after arriving at Topaz. On her way home from another block, "the wind suddenly gathered ominous strength. It swept around us in great thrusting gusts, flinging swirling masses of sand in the air and engulfing us in a thick cloud that eclipsed barracks only ten feet away." Ducking into a laundry barrack, she attempted to hide from the monstrous storm that threatened to tear the flimsy building apart. After an hour the storm had not let up, but during a brief lull Yoshiko tried to reach home. The dust nearly choked her to death and only "fear gave me strength to fight the storm."

Once, when braving another storm to get to her second-grade classroom, Yoshiko Uchida found some of her students waiting in the dust-filled room. "I was touched . . . to see their eagerness to learn despite the desolation of their surroundings, the meager tools for

The white cloud rolling across the desert just behind the barracks is an approaching dust storm.

learning, and in this case the physical dangers they encountered just to reach school." Children had a certain sense of purpose in their lives as long as they were coming to school.

Sometimes dust storms would last four days. But despite the danger and discomfort, children could still find something to laugh about: "Many times we did not have our bandanas so that the dust gathers in our hair. We would tease each other and say, 'Gee! You're an old lady or grandma.' "

The diary notes the return of Mrs. Hori (still Miss Yamauchi to her students) after her marriage. She and her fiancé, Saburo, had been permitted to travel to Fillmore, the county seat, to get their marriage license. Because cameras were not allowed in camp at that time, they had stopped in Delta to have a wedding picture taken. On Saturday, March 20, Anne and Saburo were married by a Buddhist reverend in the barrack used as a Buddhist temple. A real honeymoon would have to wait until years later.

The Boy and Girl Scout programs provided a marvelous diversion for the children interned in Topaz. Later, as camp security was relaxed, Raymond and the other scouts were allowed to leave the barbed-wire confines for camping trips. But in the early days of Topaz, the Boy Scouts played a different and more somber role. A scout band would perform at the gate to welcome the new arrivals, trying to make them feel a little better about being shipped so far from home.

April 14, 1943

On Sunday evening at 7:30 o'clock, an old man, Mr. James H. Wakasa passed away.

This morning some of our boys saw a dog balancing on a car as it drove by on the road.

Yesterday we started to build our "cookie house" for Hansel and Gretel. Edwin, Bobby, Lynn and Kei were chosen to work on it.

Today Kiku's mother and father left Topaz. His father went to Idaho and his mother went to Salt Lake City.

There was a fire at the turkey farm last night.

We went to see the ant hills, scorpions and horned toad at Miss Ito's and Mr. Kusano's class.

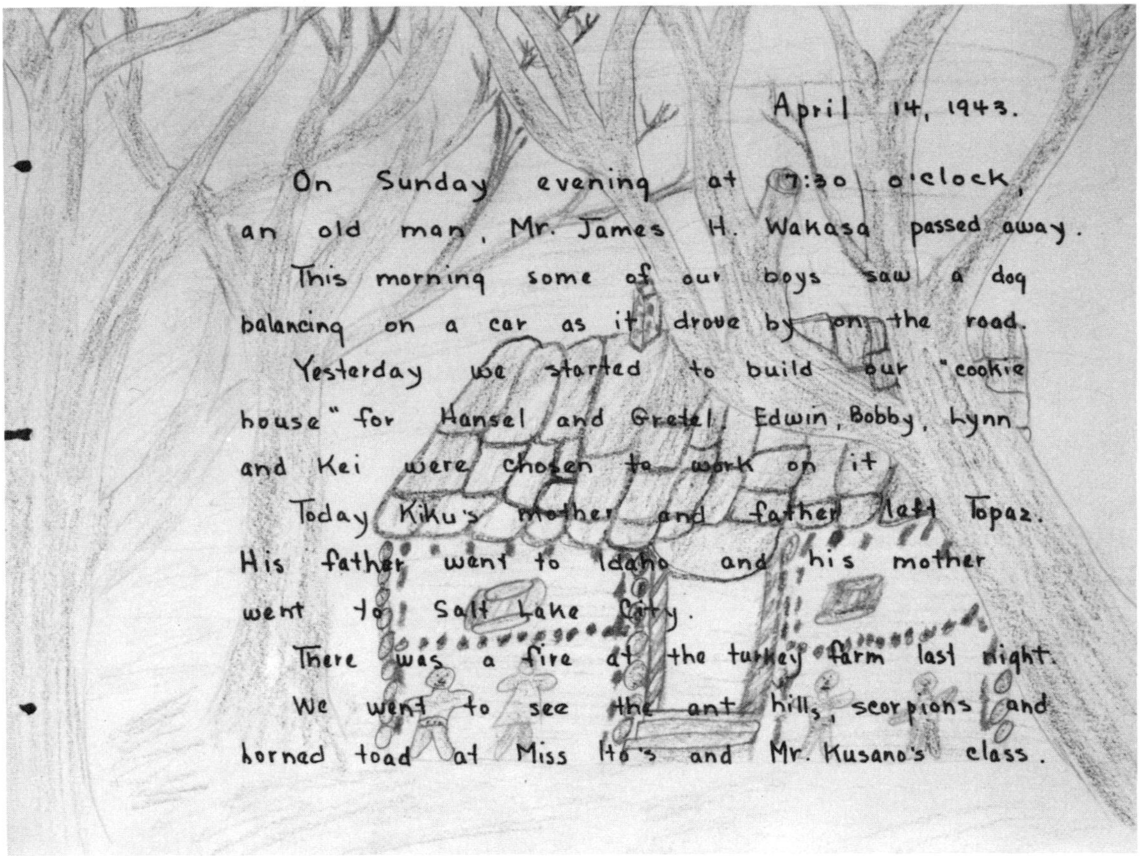

April 14, 1943.

On Sunday evening at 7:30 o'clock, an old man, Mr. James H. Wakasa passed away.

This morning some of our boys saw a dog balancing on a car as it drove by on the road.

Yesterday we started to build our "cookie house" for Hansel and Gretel. Edwin, Bobby, Lynn and Kei were chosen to work on it.

Today Kiku's mother and father left Topaz. His father went to Idaho and his mother went to Salt Lake City.

There was a fire at the turkey farm last night.

We went to see the ant hills, scorpions and horned toad at Miss Ito's and Mr. Kusano's class.

Miss Yamauchi's class mentions a number of interesting things that happened around April 14. What third grader wouldn't be quick to report seeing a dog balancing on a moving car? Or to mention a visit to see scorpions and horned toads—certainly not animals a child would find in San Francisco. The diary illustration shows the witch's gingerbread house from "Hansel and Gretel" and was probably the inspiration for the "cookie house" scenery the class made for their school play. And a fire was always big news. The turkey farm that burned was one of several farms near Topaz where internees raised food for the camp.

Why did Kiku's parents leave Topaz? It was common for internees to leave for work release—to work on sugar-beet or potato farms in Utah and Idaho or canneries in Salt Lake City. Perhaps Kiku stayed with his grandparents or an aunt and uncle while his parents were away.

But the most dramatic event the children mention is the death of James Wakasa. Mr. Wakasa was a sixty-three-year-old Issei gentleman who was probably hard of hearing. On Sunday evening, April 11, he

A nursery school story-telling circle at Topaz.

was walking near the barbed-wire fence, perhaps looking for arrow-heads or playing with a stray dog. Suddenly a shot rang out from the nearest guard tower, striking Mr. Wakasa in the chest and killing him instantly. The guard claimed that he called out four times to warn Mr. Wakasa and then fired when the elderly man tried to climb under the fence—although his body was found several feet inside the enclosure. Even if James Wakasa had been trying to escape, where would he have gone?

The shooting caused an uproar. Why didn't the guard fire a warning shot? Who was safe now? The military was put on alert, complete with machine guns and gas masks. The military police even threat-ened the internees, warning that if they didn't stay away from the site of the shooting they would "get what the other guy had gotten." In the end, the facts about Mr. Wakasa's death were covered up. The guard's name, Gerald Philpott, and background—he had just returned from fighting in the Pacific and was reportedly a "Jap-hater"—were never released to the press. The residents of Topaz were never told whether or not Philpott was punished. In fact, he was barely reprimanded and then transferred from Topaz.

The camp newspapers didn't publish the whole truth, either. Topaz administrators censored what was printed. For instance, the *Topaz Times* reported that Mr. Wakasa had tried to climb the fence. No correction of the facts was ever made, and no opinions about the event or its causes were printed.

Fear of administration control, which was backed up by all those guns, may explain why the children's diary used the calming words "passed away" to describe Mr. Wakasa's violent death. Certainly Miss Yamauchi was not trying to shield her students from the terrible truth. In a place as small and overcrowded as Topaz, keeping such a secret would have been impossible. Even young children must have known that Mr. Wakasa had been killed. Perhaps Miss Yamauchi was trying to protect the children and herself by not writing anything she thought might anger the camp officials.

April 20, 1943

There was a parade of war machines in Delta on Sunday.
Saturday, Edwin was given a little dog named "Tippy."
Today is Hitler's birthday.
Yesterday was Mr. Wakasa's funeral.

Kiku brought us four lizards today.
There was a flower show at Block 36.

According to Japanese tradition, the site of one's death is the best spot for one's funeral. The camp administration was afraid that if Mr. Wakasa's funeral was held at the fence where he was shot, there might be a riot. Finally, residents and administration compromised, and the funeral was held near the place Mr. Wakasa died but away from the fence. There were no riots, but the days before the funeral were filled with nonviolent protests. Internees stayed home from work or conducted work stoppages.

Although Mr. Wakasa had no family, nearly two thousand people attended his funeral. Afterward, the camp administration restricted the use of arms and kept soldiers who had fought the Japanese in the Pacific from being assigned to Topaz. Yet when a member of the landscape crew erected a monument to Wakasa, it was quickly removed.

Mr. Wakasa's funeral was also a way to protest his killing. A large number of camp residents attended.

The war was ever present in the children's lives, although the parade of war machines in Delta was probably off-limits to them. Still, tales of the parade inspired the young artist of this diary page, who was most likely unfamiliar with small-town Delta and therefore drew the taller buildings of a California city. And what about Hitler's birthday? Maybe the children wondered if nasty tyrants really celebrated such happy occasions.

Flower and craft shows were frequent events at Topaz and were often part of the adult education program. Because flowers were nearly impossible to grow, residents made beautiful copies from paper. The flowers at Mr. Wasaka's funeral were all made of paper. Besides flower making, adult classes included English, first aid, music, art, sewing, geography, Americanization (for the older Issei), and carpentry. The adult education division also administered and operated the Boy Scout program.

Edwin's getting a puppy was an important event, since so many beloved pets had been left behind in California. Even animals like lizards helped replace pets for some children.

May 3, 1943

Sunday there was a Buddhist parade. It is called an Hana-Matsuri parade.

Yesterday a little boy found a dollar bill in the high school grounds.

We elected our new president and vice-president. They are Kei and Betty.

Saturday Lynn, David and Don went to the gravel pit. They were so tired they waited at the pit until a truck brought them home.

There are many pupils absent lately due to an epidemic of flu in Topaz.

Christians and Buddhists were the major religious groups in the relocation camps. In Topaz about 40 percent of the residents were Protestant, 20 percent Catholic, and 40 percent Buddhist, as well as a

May 3, 1943.

Sunday there was a Buddhist parade. It is called an Hana-Matsuri parade.

Yesterday a little boy found a dollar bill in the high school grounds.

We elected our new president and vice-president. They are Kei and Betty.

Saturday Seymour Bauer and Don went to the gravel pit. They were so tired they waited at the pit until a truck brought them home.

There are many pupils absent lately due to an epidemic of flu in Topaz.

scant number from other faiths. A few Japanese Americans were Shintos. At Tanforan, Shintos were not allowed to worship because they believed the emperor of Japan was one of their many gods. Since the United States was at war with the emperor of Japan, emperor worship seemed at best unpatriotic and at worst traitorous. By the time the Nikkei arrived at Topaz, no one seemed to be Shinto. Perhaps Shintos had simply decided to worship secretly.

Hana-Matsuri is a flower festival held in honor of the birth of Buddha, whose life and teachings provide the foundation of the Buddhist religion. The festival included folk dancing and a parade. It must have been an exciting event for the children. The bright colors and festive activities were a contrast to the drab surroundings of the camp. All the flowers in the May 3 drawing, as well as the others that decorated the Hana-Matsuri celebration, were paper flowers created by the residents of the camp.

The diary mentions a flu epidemic. Some children probably had to go to the hospital, which was slow in being completed (as were the living quarters) and lacked the necessary supplies and staff. When the

The nurses and staff of Topaz Hospital.

shortages were finally filled, Nikkei doctors were still unhappy, taking orders from sometimes less skilled white doctors and making almost no money (twenty-one dollars a month). Often cases were sent to Delta or even to Salt Lake City for treatment because the hospital was understaffed or did not have the needed equipment.

May 5, 1943

Today is Japanese Boys' Day. We see many carps flying high on the roofs of barracks and dining halls.

May 6th and 7th will be our Spring Vacation. The teachers are going to have a conference.

This Sunday is Mother's Day.

All residents of Block 29 must not leave their block because of the case of Infantile Paralysis.

May 5, 1943.

Today is Japanese Boys' Day. We see
many carps flying high on the roofs of
barracks and dining halls.
    May 6th and 7th will be our Spring Vaca-
tion. The teachers are going to have a
conference.
    This Sunday is Mother's Day
    All residents of Block 29 must not leave
their block because of the case of
Infantile Paralysis.

Japanese Boys' Day is a traditional Japanese festival that dates back hundreds of years. The celebration honors the sons in each family. From poles raised in yards or on roofs, hollow cloth or paper streamers shaped like carp (a type of fish) are flown like flags. The carp symbolizes strength, courage, and determination. In the drawing for May 5, there are two fish streamers flying above the barrack. The largest carp, generally at the top, stands for the oldest son. The streamers get shorter (and usually lower on the pole) according to the ages of a family's other sons.

Traditionally, a family would set out items that reminded boys of their Japanese heritage and of strength and courage: armor, helmets, and swords once used by family members or tiny dolls arranged to show scenes from Japanese hero stories. The sword-shaped leaves of the iris plant, another symbol of strength, often were soaked in bathwater before the boys bathed. Also, for good luck and strength, boys ate rice wrapped in iris, bamboo, and oak leaves. Because military equipment, such as swords, was forbidden in the camp, and because families didn't want to appear *too* Japanese, some of these traditions were altered or toned down.

[34]

In the diary entry, we are told that carp also were flown from the roofs of the dining halls. Notice that the children did not say "mess halls." The administrators at Topaz thought that using the term "dining hall" would make the camp seem less like an internment or detention center. The moment new arrivals entered the gates, they were handed an instruction sheet that read, "Here we say Dining Hall and not Mess Hall; Safety Council, not Internal Police; Residents, not Evacuees; and last but not least, Mental Climate, not Morale."

Infantile paralysis, or poliomyelitis, was a dreaded disease for which there was no vaccine in 1943. Polio is contagious and affects mostly children. It can cripple or kill. When someone in a neighborhood, such as Block 29, was diagnosed with polio, everyone—especially children—stayed indoors. Keeping away from someone or something that contained the polio virus was the only way to prevent getting the disease. And in a place like Topaz, where eight thousand people were crammed into one square mile, it was even more difficult to avoid being infected. A polio outbreak must have been terrifying for Miss Yamauchi's third graders. Fortunately, there is now a vaccine to prevent polio.

Like Japanese Boys' Day, Kabuki was another traditional event staged in Topaz. Kabuki is a form of Japanese theater that combines mask-like makeup and elaborate costumes with dance, music, and melodrama.

May 17, 1943.

Last Saturday and Sunday there was an airplane contest in the high school grounds.

Friday was "Play Day" for high school students. There was so much mud and rough playing that some people were hurt. Lynn's father captured the "Faculty Flag".

This morning signs were put up showing the names of the streets of Topaz.

Makoto went to see his father at the cattle ranch. Makoto was very lucky because he rode on a horse. All the boys in our class would surely love to ride a horse!

Kiku's auntie came from Arkansas.

May 17, 1943

Last Saturday and Sunday there was an airplane contest in the high school grounds.

Friday was "Play Day" for high school students. There was so much mud and rough playing that some people were hurt. Lynn's father captured the "Faculty Flag."

This morning signs were put up showing the names of the streets of Topaz.

Makoto went to see his father at the cattle ranch. Makoto was very lucky because he rode on a horse. All the boys in our class would surely love to ride a horse!

Kiku's auntie came from Arkansas.

School was an important event for the younger children in Topaz. And high-school activities, such as football games and "Play Day," provided entertainment for old and young alike, as did the model airplane contest mentioned in the diary. However, living in a relocation camp environment quickly changed how small children viewed life. Yoshiko Uchida noticed the change in Tanforan while she was teaching nursery school.

> Whenever the children played house, they always stood in line to eat at make-believe mess halls rather than cooking and setting tables as they would have done at home. It was sad to see how quickly the concept of home had changed for them.

Since the camp was like a maze, the inhabitants of Topaz welcomed their new street signs. Residents, especially children, would get lost because every place in camp looked the same. Each residential block had identical buildings, arranged in identical ways. People who were lost must have felt like they were walking in circles, never getting closer to home. At least the signs provided some way to tell one street and one area of camp from another. The streets were named for plants and minerals found in the environment near Topaz—names like Sage Street, Greasewood Way, and Agate Avenue.

The cattle ranch was another of Topaz's nearby agricultural operations that supplied the internees with food. Within a few miles of the camp, there also were a hog farm, a nursery, a chicken farm, and the

No matter what the camp administrators called them, the dining halls were nothing more than army-style mess halls.

This is how the classrooms looked when the school barracks were finally completed.

turkey farm mentioned earlier. Makoto's trip to visit his father, who worked at the cattle ranch, was a treat. Who wouldn't want a chance to escape the barbed wire for a little while and ride a horse?

Even though the relocation camps limited the internees' freedom, the residents did have a few "privileges." One such "privilege" was the opportunity to transfer from one camp to another to be with family. Kiku's auntie must have come to Topaz from the relocation camp in Rohwer or Jerome, Arkansas.

May 18, 1943

We have a large box filled with nails. Every day we bring more and more nails for Uncle Sam.

Yesterday a big bomber flew over Topaz.

Our paper folders tear so easily that we have decided to pay 8¢ each for some material to make new folders.

Edwin brought us a baby horned toad. It is now living with our five lizards.

[38]

Kimiko's mother was burned very badly by hot water. Yesterday little Drayton Nuttall found Don's money. Don was surely happy to have it returned.

May 18, 1943.

We have a large box filled with nails. Every day we bring more and more nails for Uncle Sam.

Yesterday a big bomber flew over Topaz. Our paper folders tear so easily that we have decided to pay 8¢ each for some material to make new folders.

Edwin brought us a baby horned toad. It is now living with our five lizards.

Kimiko's mother was burned very badly by hot water.

Yesterday little Drayton Nuttall found Don's money. Don was surely happy to have it returned.

During World War II, Americans who were not away fighting pitched in to help the war effort by recycling anything and everything that could be turned into guns, tanks, parachutes, or other war materials. Nails were made of steel, which could be used for all sorts of war-related items. It was not much of a sacrifice for Americans outside the relocation camps to save old nails for the government, but nails were scarce and valuable to the Japanese Americans. They collected and straightened nails from the boxes and crates that came into camp and used them to build furniture and shelves. The barracks were bare, except for army cots and coal stoves, so everything else had to be made from whatever scrap wood was available. It was a patriotic sacrifice for the Nikkei to save nails for Uncle Sam, as the young artist has indicated with a border of bent nails surrounding crossed American flags.

What could Don and the other children use their money for in Topaz? Though residents were provided with room and board, other services and sources of entertainment were not free. Residents used money to mail letters and packages from the Topaz Post Office. They also spent money at a variety of businesses that began to appear in the camp within the first few weeks. The businesses were owned and operated as a consumers' cooperative by the internees themselves. The Co-op started with the Canteen (like a snack bar) and then expanded to include two movie houses, a barbershop, a radio repair shop, and a dry goods store. The dry goods store, much like a small department store, was such a hit that it brought in $2,700 on its opening day (a large sum for a small community of people making very little money). Later, the Co-op even operated a photo service. From time to time, internees were allowed a pass to go into Delta to shop. Because the government food budget for the camps was only thirty-nine cents a day per person (later it dropped to thirty-one cents with restrictions on milk and coffee), the Nikkei enjoyed going into Delta to buy tasty snacks to enhance the mess hall offerings. Ted Nagata, who was in kindergarten when he entered Topaz, remembers being in heaven when he was able to go to the Canteen and buy a "Coke and a Baby Ruth."

Hot water was not always plentiful in the public washing and bathing facilities, especially in the early days of Topaz. When it was available, people rushed to wash clothes or shower. Yoshiko Uchida remembered that "the showers were difficult to adjust and we either got scalded by torrents of hot water or shocked by an icy blast of cold." Kimiko's mother may have been burned by the unpredictable water in her block.

With the rain, the dusty Topaz streets were transformed into quagmires. Residents dropped boards in the mud to create rough sidewalks. It's dry here, so these two young girls avoid the "sidewalk" on their way to the Canteen.

May 19, 1943.

Today Miss Kushida's class and our class played baseball.

Kei received a new sweater and two books from his grandmother.

Last night Don and Robert helped the people of their block. They stacked fire wood until 10:30 P.M. They are very tired today.

Today Miss Yamauchi told us a story about snakes.

A man at Block 23 was running and he suddenly fell forward in a faint.

Betty's sister was lost but she was found wandering around in another block. Each block is so much alike that it is easy to get lost.

May 19, 1943

Today Miss Kushida's class and our class played baseball.

Kei received a new sweater and two books from his grandmother.

Last night Don and Robert helped the people of their block. They stacked fire wood until 10:30 P.M. They are very tired today.

Today Miss Yamauchi told us a story about snakes.

A man at Block 23 was running and he suddenly fell forward in a faint.

Betty's sister was lost but she was found wandering around in another block. Each block is so much alike that it is easy to get lost.

Teachers like Miss Kushida and Miss Yamauchi were paid $19 a month, while the white teachers in Topaz were paid a regular teaching salary of $150 to $200 a month, plus room and board. The Japanese Americans were a classless society in Topaz, so wages only varied from $16 to $21 (not to exceed the minimum wage for a private in the U.S. Army). Even though many internees had money in banks back home, the government froze the accounts, making most of their money unavailable. And if internees worked outside of camp and earned regular, higher wages, they were made to pay rent to live in Topaz.

Because of a teacher shortage, many of the Nikkei instructors, although college graduates, were not trained teachers. Miss Yamauchi, however, had graduated from the University of California at Berkeley with a teaching degree. For some reason, the small number of white teachers all were kept at Mountain View School, which was located close to the administration buildings and their living quarters. Desert View was staffed entirely by Japanese-American teachers.

This famous photograph of four Nisei college girls in front of Sather Gate, entrance to the University of California at Berkeley campus, hangs in the Smithsonian Institute. From left to right are Takako Tsuchiya (Anne's best friend), Miyuki Kusumine, Lillian "Anne" Yamauchi, and Michi Yamazaki. *Takako Endo*

Sports programs were an important diversion in Topaz. Football, baseball, basketball, and even sumo wrestling were popular. The high-school teams would play teams from nearby public schools. And not only the players enjoyed the games. All the sports events drew crowds of spectators—real fans! With their own funds, internees also stocked Recreation Barracks with equipment for Ping-Pong, badminton, and other indoor activities.

Baseball was the most popular of these pastimes; some of the internees even felt that baseball kept them from going crazy in the camps. Children in elementary school, high-school students, and adults all had their teams. Popular as it was, baseball was also responsible for plenty of accidents. Throughout the pages of the diary, the children report other children being hit and injured by balls and bats.

Besides sports, there were little things that made life exciting, such as Kei getting presents from his grandmother or a man fainting in the street. And the mention of someone getting lost right in Topaz shows up more than once in the diary. Even with the newly installed street signs, youngsters like Betty's sister and also adults still had trouble finding their way.

Baseball was a popular sport among the Japanese Americans well before World War II. This photograph of a Nikkei team from Salt Lake City was taken the summer before Pearl Harbor.

May 21, 1943

Yesterday Edwin fed some bread crumbs to hungry seagulls.

Harry brought a telescope to school today. Everyone wanted to look through it. Even boys and girls from other classes formed a line for their turn to peek through Harry's telescope.

This afternoon the second group of the Japanese American Combat team left Topaz to join Uncle Sam's army. Edwin's uncle is a volunteer too.

At Block 16, the chimney of the boiler room puffed smoke rings, just like a man smoking a cigarette.

Edwin and the other Nikkei probably were surprised to find seagulls so far from the ocean. Because of Great Salt Lake, which sits about a hundred miles north of Topaz, the large white birds are commonplace in much of Utah. The gulls must have seemed like visitors from home to these children from the Bay Area of California.

In the diary, Miss Yamauchi's class tells about young men leaving to join "Uncle Sam's army." But immediately after Pearl Harbor, no Nisei was drafted or allowed to volunteer for the military. Those already serving were discharged. Or they were reassigned to some place "safe" and given "safe" tasks—typing, kitchen duty, janitorial work. Finally, early in 1943, President Roosevelt approved a plan to create an all-Nisei combat unit, the 442nd Regimental Combat Team. "No loyal citizen of the United States should be denied the democratic right to exercise the responsibilities of his citizenship, regardless of his ancestry," said the president.

The news that the government wanted Nisei boys to serve was met with mixed reactions in the camps. Some didn't like the idea of a segregated combat unit; others thought such a unit would give the Japanese Americans a chance to stand out and show the country Nisei loyalty. However, when recruiters came to the camps to sign up volunteers, they were surprised to find that the young men were not especially enthusiastic. The loyalty oaths asking them to renounce any loyalty to the Japanese emperor infuriated the Nisei. After all, they thought, we are native-born, loyal Americans who have never felt allegiance to the emperor, like some of our parents. The first recruiting attempt produced only a third of what the government expected, about 1,200 volunteers from all the camps. At Topaz, 113 young men volunteered. The army accepted 59 of them for military service.

A year later, January 1, 1944, the government decided to draft the Japanese Americans. By that time, some of the Nisei were so disillusioned with the United States that they refused to go. Taken from their homes, kept in camps in the wilderness—why should they fight for the United States? But the government wasn't sympathetic. In July, sixty-three men from the camp at Heart Mountain, Wyoming, were convicted of resisting the draft and sentenced to three years in the federal penitentiary. But despite strong resistance to the draft by some, the attitudes of many young Nisei shifted by the spring of 1944, and more were willing to go. The fact that several hundred young Nisei women were taken into the Women's Auxiliary Army Corps (later, the WAC) helped stimulate men to volunteer—they didn't want to seem less patriotic.

The 442nd Regimental Combat Team was an elite unit. The IQs of its men were higher than the requirement for officer training programs, and their intelligence and bravery were soon apparent. The motto of the 442nd was "Go for Broke," and that's just what they did. They had one of the highest casualty rates in the Army (9,000 dead or wounded) because of their daring and impossible feats. In the end, the 442nd, which was combined with the 100th Infantry Battalion made up of Japanese Americans from Hawaii, was the most decorated unit in the war. They received 18,143 medals and citations, enough for two units.

An example of their fighting spirit is the story of the "lost battalion." A unit from Texas was surrounded by Germans in the French countryside. No one could get through, then the 442nd arrived. They rescued the Texans, but not without a price. The 442nd suffered a 60 percent casualty rate, losing more men than the three hundred they saved.

Nisei were also sent to the Pacific to fight the Japanese. They were used mostly as interpreters and scouts. But when the army tried to find Nisei who could speak Japanese, they were shocked to discover that they were so Americanized that only 10 percent knew the language well enough. Young Japanese Americans who spoke fluent Japanese were often Kibei (*Key-bay*), Nisei whose parents had sent them to Japan for a year or two of schooling.

Nisei soldiers became the secret weapon in the Pacific, because the Japanese military was so sure that the Americans could not understand their language. They sent messages without putting them into code, and the Japanese Americans easily translated them. But a Kibei serviceman named Kenny Yasui did more than translate messages. He

Young Nisei men home on leave before being shipped off to fight in Europe. Ironically, these U.S. servicemen had to visit their families in barbed-wire enclosures.

pretended to be a Japanese colonel and captured sixteen enemy soldiers by ordering them to drop their weapons and march to his orders.

The valor of the Nisei soldiers did much to change American public opinion about the Japanese Americans. Yet, when Ernest Uno returned home from combat, not only did he find his mother still in a camp, but his reunion with her was conducted in the presence of an armed guard.

May 24, 1943.

Many people left Topaz this afternoon for the "Tent City" in Provo, Utah. They will pick strawberries, cherries, apples and peaches. Grace's big brother was one of the workers. Edwin's uncle will have to leave a little later because his auntie had a brand new baby.

On Saturday night there was a Boy Scout Program at Dining Hall 32.

Today we started a frieze about shelter.

Last Saturday a dog had a fight with a porcupine. The poor dog had porcupine quills all over his body.

Yesterday, Don's mother came home from the hospital. Don may leave Topaz soon.

May 24, 1943

Many people left Topaz this afternoon for the "Tent City" in Provo, Utah. They will pick strawberries, cherries, apples and peaches. Grace's big brother was one of the workers. Edwin's uncle will have to leave a little later because his auntie had a brand new baby.

On Saturday night there was a Boy Scout Program at Dining Hall 32.

Today we started a frieze about shelter.

[47]

Last Saturday a dog had a fight with a porcupine. The poor dog had porcupine quills all over his body.

Yesterday, Don's mother came home from the hospital. Don may leave Topaz soon.

As noted earlier, internees were frequently in and out of Topaz for a variety of temporary work opportunities. The residents of Topaz often jumped at the chance to get away from the monotony of the camp and to make better wages. Because many men and women were off fighting the war, America suffered from labor shortages. Therefore, the Japanese Americans in the relocation camps were hired to provide much needed help.

The "Tent City" in Provo, Utah, about ninety miles from Delta, was erected to house residents from Topaz who wanted to work picking fruit. The orchards around Provo produced strawberries, cherries, apples, and peaches—all of which are pictured by the artist on the diary page for May 24. The laborers from Topaz picked strawberries first because they "came on" around the end of May. Then cherries in June, apricots in July, peaches and pears in September, and apples in October.

At first, those who went to Provo were met with some hostility. The local Woolworth and J.C. Penney stores would not sell to the Japanese Americans, and some restaurants wouldn't serve them.

Many Topaz residents went north to pick the fruit crops in Utah Valley. This mother and daughter relax in their temporary home, a "tent city" in Provo, Utah.

Toughs harassed and mistreated Nikkei who were alone or in small groups, and some were stoned while riding in trucks back and forth from work. At one point, Tent City was attacked with rifle fire. Two buildings were struck by fifteen to eighteen rifle rounds while the Nikkei residents hugged the floors. The camp manager, H. W. Bartlett, was convinced that the shots were aimed at the Japanese Americans. Later, five teenagers were arrested for "terrorism." Whether the citizens of Provo decided that Nikkei labor was necessary for the war effort or whether they truly were fighting prejudice is unclear, but a group of local people came to the Japanese Americans' rescue. They condemned the violence and promised better law enforcement and "tolerant participation in the democratic spirit." Still, many of the workers from Topaz never felt completely safe.

In the diary, the children tell about working on a frieze (probably like a mural) for a class project. Art was stressed in the elementary classrooms of Topaz and was usually worked into social studies, writing, and other subjects. For instance, this diary was a project illustrated by the students.

The poor dog that tangled (and lost the battle) with a porcupine was probably one of the many stray dogs that began to collect around the camp. Wild animals, such as coyotes, also fought with the dogs. In fact, coyotes would come right into Topaz, especially during the winter, to scavenge for food. Sometimes residents found several hungry and fearless coyotes lurking just outside their barracks doors.

May 26, 1943

Don is going to leave for Logan to help on the farm. We shall all miss him very much.

We have a new American flag for our room.

Yesterday Bobby lost his sling shot because he was in such a hurry to deliver the "Topaz Times" for his Block Manager.

The Military Police beat the Administration by the score of 11 to 5. At Block 30, the little boys played baseball against the old men. The little boys won, 21 to 10.

Lynn is going to have a new brother or sister very very soon.

Today Johnny's sister left for Idaho to be with her fiancé.

May 26, 1943.

Don is going to leave for Logan to help on the farm. We shall all miss him very much.

We have a new American flag for our room.

Yesterday Bobby lost his sling shot because he was in such a hurry to deliver the "Topaz Times" for his Block Manager.

The Military Police beat the Administration by the score of 11 to 5. At Block 30, the little boys played baseball against the old men. The little boys won, 21 to 10.

Lynn is going to have a new brother or sister very very soon.

Today Johnny's sister left for Idaho to be with her fiancé.

The first groups to arrive from Tanforan immediately got to work on the *Topaz Times*. The first edition of the camp newspaper was delivered to the internees in Yoshiko Uchida's group before they stepped off the train in Delta. She remembered the paper contained "instructions regarding procedures for camp life." The *Topaz Times* was published in English and Japanese three times a week.

Although a camp paper might have sprung to life on its own, the truth is that the War Relocation Authority ordered that a newspaper be published in each relocation center. The *Topaz Times* was written by the internees but controlled by the government. Instead of openly censoring the paper, the camp authorities carefully chose the newspaper staff so that the news was indirectly controlled. Even when James Wakasa was shot and killed, the *Topaz Times* did the bidding of the camp director and printed inaccurate accounts. However, there was a time when the Japanese edition of the paper advised camp residents to resist orders from the administration. The *Times* staff members who took part in this behavior were forced to resign, and new translators were hired who would make sure the Japanese version matched the English version. But, controlled as it was, the *Topaz*

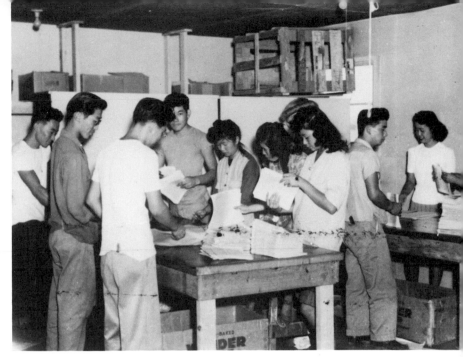

The circulation staff of the *Topaz Times* prepares the camp newspaper for delivery.

Times was a welcome communicator. Happy news items such as baseball scores, birth announcements, and notices of camp activities filled most of the space.

Bobby, the boy in Miss Yamauchi's class who lost his slingshot, was a *Times* paperboy for his block manager. Block managers were appointed by the administration and paid sixteen dollars a month. They saw to the needs of 250 to 300 people, including delivering the *Topaz Times*. Managers also provided brooms, lightbulbs, and soap and made sure their blocks were well maintained.

Along with the appointment of block managers, the War Relocation Authority established community councils at Topaz and other camps as an experiment in self-government. The Authority called for the election of a representative from each block to serve on the council. At first, the administration wouldn't allow the Issei to run for office because they weren't U.S. citizens. That meant that the Nisei held the positions on the council, and that didn't sit well with their elders.

These elected representatives were supposed to govern the residents in the camps, but the Nikkei quickly realized that the community councils had no real authority. The camps were run by the white administration, and that was all there was to it. For this reason, residents' enthusiasm for the councils waned; in some camps, the councils lasted only about a year. Although the community council continued to exist in Topaz, the block manager became the more important and influential go-between for the people and the admin-

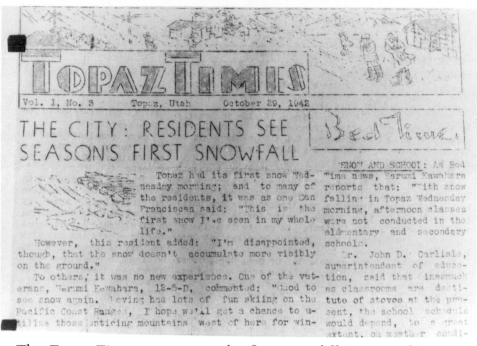

The *Topaz Times* announces the first snowfall in camp history. Many of the Nikkei from the West Coast had never seen snow before.

istration. The managers were not meant to be a governing body, like the council, but were simply employees of the War Relocation Authority.

Once again, the children talk of baseball in their diary—lots of teams playing one another regularly. And they mention here, and often in other entries, that new babies were being born into camp life. In fact, during the days of the Topaz Relocation Center, there were 384 births and only 139 deaths.

June 24, 1943

The seniors of the Topaz High School will hold their Graduation Exercises on June 25, 1943. They will all wear caps and gowns.

Miss Yamauchi's brother, Dr. Paul Yamauchi will be married this Saturday night.

Kiku wrote us a letter today telling us how busy he is riding horses and irrigating his farm in Idaho. He promised us some candy too.

[52]

Tomorrow is the last day of school. After a weeks vaca-
tion, we shall all meet again at 32-4-CD for Summer School.
We wrote "thank you" letters to the High Fourth Grade
for their invitation to "The Trials of Queen Violetta."

June 24, 1943.

The seniors of the Topaz High School will hold their Graduation Exercises on June 25, 1943. They will all wear caps and gowns.

Miss Yamauchi's brother, Dr. Paul Yamauchi will be married this Saturday night.

Kiku wrote us a letter today telling us how busy he is riding horses and irrigating his farm in Idaho. He promised us some candy too.

Tomorrow is the last day of school. After a weeks vacation, we shall all meet again at 32-4-CD for Summer School.

We wrote "thank you" letters to the High Fourth Grade for their invitation to "The Trials of Queen Violetta".

High-school students had a more difficult time adjusting and being happy in Topaz than their elementary-age brothers and sisters. They were old enough to understand the enormous injustice of relocation. The patriotic ideals that surfaced in Miss Yamauchi's class were harder for high-school teachers to pass off on their students, who were more likely to feel bitter about their internment. "I sometimes pinch myself, am I really in Utah," said one Topaz High student, "or is this California, do I live in a barrack with other people and have only 2 rooms, not 7 or 8 I used to live in, are we going to school learning a new system, which seems odd to me, and do we have teachers of our own race, do we go to school in barracks and then I pinch myself once, twice and then I am out of my daze."

[53]

Eleanor Gerard Sekerak said that her students at Topaz High School participated in "all the normal life of a typical high school," including a "student chorus, student newspaper, yearbook, student government, drama, athletics . . . dances, and the usual senior week activities." However, students found the segregated atmosphere unsettling. Seeing virtually all Japanese faces around them in school was unlike anything any of them had experienced before the war. Though Sekerak was remembered fondly by her students as someone who tried to make up for the wrongs of internment, many students thought the schools and teachers were inferior and felt unprepared to go on to college. The class of 1943 probably had the most positive experience of all the senior classes to graduate from Topaz. The camp schools were at their best that first year but steadily weakened after that. Good teachers left and were hard to replace, and school facilities never really improved. As resident morale began to sag, many young people became bored and disrespectful—unusual behavior for Japanese-American students.

On June 16, Kiku Kitow, one of Miss Yamauchi's students, moved with his family to a farm in Idaho. Later, in the diary entry for July 6, the children reported that Kiku, true to his word, sent them two boxes of candy.

Resettlement outside the camps was actually encouraged by the War Relocation Authority. A few Nikkei moved in with relatives who were living far enough inland from the West Coast. But most Japanese Americans either did not have places to go or found it harder than expected to get the final clearance to leave Topaz.

Seniors pass under the "arms" of a block "T" and step up to receive their diplomas from Topaz High School.

Miss Yamauchi's students seemed to do a lot of letter writing in school, such as the letters they wrote thanking the High Fourth Grade for the invitation to their class play. In other diary entries, the children mention writing several other thank-you letters, invitations to class activities, and letters to third- and fourth-grade classes in Delta. In fact, when Miss Yamauchi was away from her class for a few days, the students wrote letters to her.

> July 5, 1943.
>
> It is the first day of Summer School. We start at 8:30 and are dismissed at 11:30 A.M.
>
> There was a camp-wide 4th of July carnival on the week-end of July 3rd and 4th. It was lots of fun.
>
> The Boy Scouts went camping for one week yesterday.
>
> Edwin went to the Pig farm every day for one week to help feed the pigs.
>
> Yesterday was the Fourth of July.
>
> A fire extinguisher saved a barrack from catching on fire when some careless children threw sparklers on the roof.

July 5, 1943

It is the first day of Summer School. We start at 8:30 and are dismissed at 11:30 A.M.

There was a camp-wide 4th of July carnival on the week-end of July 3rd and 4th. It was lots of fun.

The Boy Scouts went camping for one week yesterday.

Edwin went to the Pig farm every day for one week to help feed the pigs.

Yesterday was the Fourth of July.
A fire extinguisher saved a barrack from catching on fire
when some careless children threw sparklers on the roof.

Parents in Topaz probably loved summer school. It kept their children, who were already restless in their one-square-mile world, occupied. It also gave classes the chance to do summer activities together, such as growing a victory garden.

Another summer pastime for students was reading, and Topaz had a fine library to provide the books, no thanks to the government. Topaz Library started with a donation of five thousand volumes from friends and schools in California. Librarians charged small rental fees on best-sellers and minimal fines on overdue books to raise money to buy new items. Library notes and book reviews began to appear in the *Topaz Times*. The library finally moved into a 20-by-100-foot area in Block 16, half for adults, half for children. Another library that held only Japanese language books was located in Block 40. The Salt Lake

People across America planted victory gardens to help the war effort. The idea behind the small garden plots was to make American families grow their own food. The food that they'd normally get from farms could then be sent overseas to the fighting men and women. Topaz residents, including school classes, were no less patriotic. Here a class prepares a garden spot.

County Library System started lending titles to the Topaz Library on a rotating basis, and the University of California at Berkeley and the Utah college libraries began to offer interlibrary loan services. Finally, funding from the WRA provided a budget for magazine subscriptions.

Few would have blamed the residents of Topaz if they had decided to ignore the Fourth of July in protest. The meaning of Independence Day no longer seemed to apply to eight thousand souls in the Utah desert. But instead, the whole weekend was turned into a celebration—a regular carnival complete with sparklers that almost burned down a barrack!

Edwin Narahara always seems to have something to tell the class. His name appears in the diary more than anyone else's. Today, over fifty years later, Edwin says he's forgotten a lot about his stay in Topaz. But he remembers being allowed to play on the government land that surrounded the camp. Even though the Topaz living area was fenced in and was only one square mile, the government acquired about 17,000 acres in and around the camp (a square mile is only 640 acres). The poultry farm and cattle ranch were within the government boundaries and technically part of Topaz Relocation Center. Edwin also remembers his stint at the pig farm. He says it would take him a good two hours to walk home after feeding the pigs. Of course, the farm was only about three miles away, so Edwin may have taken a few detours along the way.

July 12, 1943

Ben was playing hardball. He missed the ball and now he has a black-eye.

James Yamasaki and Kei's father came home together from the Salt Lake Hospital.

A boy was playing with a knife and he stuck his little friend in the toe. We are going to be careful about playing with knives.

The Boy Scouts came home from camping yesterday. They were so sun-burned it was hard to tell who was who. Grace's brother was their Life-Guard.

All the little boys in Jackie's block team received red base-ball caps.

July 12, 1943.

Ben was playing hardball. He missed the ball and now he has a black-eye.

James Yamasaki and Kei's father came home together from the Salt Lake Hospital.

A boy was playing with a knife and he stuck his little friend in the toe. We are going to be careful about playing with knives.

The Boy Scouts came home from camping yesterday. They were so sun-burned it was hard to tell who was who. Grace's brother was their Life-Guard.

All the little boys in Jackie's block team received red baseball caps.

Injuries and illnesses headline the July 12 diary entry. As mentioned earlier, baseball was popular but dangerous. Kids in Topaz and all over the country played another dangerous game called Splits. Two people stand apart, facing one another, each with a pocketknife. The object is to throw the knives out to the side of each player, causing them to stick in the ground. Players must stretch their legs to reach the knife blades until one is unable to stretch far enough. The boy mentioned in the diary probably was playing Splits and missed.

As noted earlier, the Boy Scouts were very active in Topaz. In fact, it may have been a more exciting location for scouting than the cities of California. Topaz scouts were close to places in the mountains that were approved by the administration for trips and that were perfect for camp-outs.

Camping was popular partly because the scouts and their counselors liked to get up into the mountains where there were some trees. Topaz was so barren trees didn't grow. The administrators and the residents tried planting them. They ordered 10,000 seedlings, 7,500 small trees, and 75 large ones, hoping the trees eventually would control the dust and cool the camp in the summer. But instead of trees eliminating the dust, "the dust eliminated the trees." Even today no trees exist on the site of Topaz—only greasewood shrubs.

The boys in Miss Yamauchi's class were too young for the Boy Scouts, but many were Cub Scouts. And many younger girls were Brownies who were looking forward to the Girl Scouts. But even without scouting, the younger children had chances to go on excursions to the desert and sometimes to the mountains with their teachers or other adults. They would find and collect rock and plant specimens and have the chance to climb trees and play out in the open. They would search for arrowheads and the fossils of trilobites, prehistoric marine animals that lived in the ancient lake that once covered Utah. These field trips often included trips to the Topaz farms.

Scouting was an important institution at Topaz.

July 20, 1943

It is Betty's birthday today. She is 9 years old. We sang "Happy Birthday" to her.

Lynn's father caught a rattlesnake at Antelope Springs. He caught it with his bare hands. It is being shown at the Hobby Show in the new Industrial Arts building.

The girls of our class will knit small squares of yarn. After we finish many many pieces, we shall put them all together and make a blanket for the American Red Cross.

July 20, 1943.

It is Betty's birthday today. She is
9 years old. We sang "Happy Birthday"
to her.

Lynn's father caught a rattle snake at
Antelope Springs. He caught it with his bare
hands. It is being shown at the Hobby Show
in the new Industrial Arts building.

The girls of our class will knit small
squares of yarn. After we finish many
many pieces, we shall put them all together and make a blanket for the
American Red Cross.

"Delta was an oasis in the midst of the alkali Pahvant Desert . . . ," said
Eleanor Gerard Sekerak. "With a sudden crack of wind, the dust storms
seemed to whirl up and around in a blinding fury . . . One simply
learned to endure dust and mud. However, other aspects of the high
desert country made up for the unpleasant ones—the wonderful silhou-
ette of Mt. Swazey on the horizon, the enticing sparkle of Topaz Mountain, the clarity of the stars at night, and the scent of sage after rain."
Rattlesnakes and scorpions were another of the unpleasant factors
Eleanor Sekerak might have mentioned. Yet, the young artist who illustrated this diary page catches a little of the mountain desert majesty
described by Mrs. Sekerak. The purple mountain in the picture probably represents Mount Swasey, a mighty landmark towering to the
west of the Topaz site.

Though it seems from this and other of the diary pages that everyone was well-adjusted and reasonably happy, it was not so. The internees worried about their future. They were often overwhelmed by
hopeless feelings or by anger over the loss of their rights. And their
cramped, uncomfortable living quarters caused family quarrels. In
fact, the traditional, strong Japanese families began to break down

because of the pressures of camp living. Even mess hall dining, rather than private family meals, contributed to this problem. Many of the young Nikkei began to show disrespect for adults and for authority in general. Gangs of juvenile delinquents appeared, shocking the administration and parents alike. Before Pearl Harbor, the Issei almost never had seen this sort of behavior from Japanese-American teenagers—talking back, cheating, committing vandalism, bullying younger children, gate-crashing parties. And although crime began to surface in camp (on May 31 the children reported that Recreational Hall 29 was robbed), Topaz had less trouble than the other relocation centers. Camp security was handled by the internees—an evacuee police force under the leadership of a government security officer. But there were so few problems that neither a jail nor a detention center existed at Topaz.

Once again, the diary tells about the amazing patriotic spirit of the interned Japanese Americans. The third-grade girls in Miss Yamauchi's class work on an afghan, a blanket made of knitted squares, to send to the American Red Cross. The Red Cross, in turn, put their donated blanket into the hands of an American serviceman.

Residents created Japanese gardens in an effort to counteract the harshness of the desert. Notice the homemade radio antenna—a cross with a net of wires—extending from one of the windows.

August 10, 1943.

Tomorrow the Brownie Club is going to Antelope Springs for a day. Six girls will go. We wish them a happy time.

Richard, Makoto, Raymond, Kaoru, George, Shizuko and Miss Yamauchi are going to Tule Center.

We are starting our letters to Mr. Ernst. We shall give him three sheetrock carvings.

Some carpenters tore down our porch. They are fixing our room all over.

August 10, 1943

Tomorrow the Brownie Club is going to Antelope Springs for a day. Six girls will go. We wish them a happy time.

Richard, Makoto, Raymond, Kaoru, George, Shizuko and Miss Yamauchi are going to Tule Center.

We are starting our letter to Mr. Ernst. We shall give him three sheetrock carvings.

Some carpenters tore down our porch. They are fixing our room all over.

Sad news appears on this diary page. Miss Yamauchi and six of her students were forced to leave Topaz for the Tule Lake Segregation Center. This happened because a loyalty questionnaire similar to that required of the Nisei soldiers was required for all camp residents seventeen years and older. Anyone not answering properly was labeled disloyal and sent to a prison camp in Tule Lake, California, so as not to pollute the minds of loyal Japanese Americans. Tule Lake was

[62]

surrounded by an eight-foot barbed-wire fence (Topaz's was only about five feet), was guarded by as many as a thousand soldiers, and had six tanks ranging the perimeter.

The questionnaire was titled "Application for Leave Clearance." As mentioned earlier, the War Relocation Authority wanted the internees to relocate to communities throughout the United States, other than those on the West Coast. Many young people qualified and were granted leave to attend universities or to work at regular jobs. But the questionnaire caused unexpected problems, mostly because of two questions borrowed directly from the army recruiters. Question 27, intended for draft-age males, read, "Are you willing to serve in the armed forces of the United States, in combat duty, wherever ordered?" Question 28 asked, "Will you swear unqualified allegiance to the United States of America and faithfully defend the United States from any and all attack by foreign or domestic forces, and forswear any form of allegiance or obedience to the Japanese emperor, or any other foreign government, power, or organization?" A response of "no-no" resulted in being sent to Tule Lake.

Residents read far more into the poorly worded questions than the government intended. Their reactions differed widely. Some men answered "no-no" because they feared they'd be drafted. Many Nisei answered "no-no" to protest the denial of their rights. Question 28 generated "no" answers from some Nisei because they felt an impor-

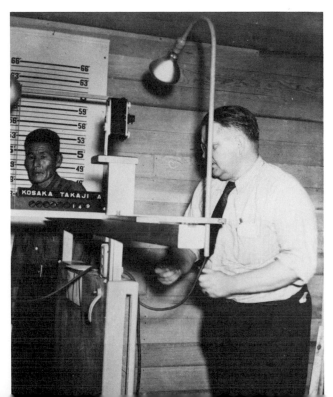

Kosaka Takaji was deemed disloyal to the United States after answering a loyalty questionnaire. He was processed like a criminal and sent to Tule Lake Segregation Center.

tant principle was involved. For instance, Togo Tanaka asked how he could renounce allegiance to the emperor when he never owed him any in the first place. So he answered "no." Some thought that Question 28 might be just such a "trap" question: if you answered "no," it revealed you *had been* loyal to the emperor. The Issei, on the other hand, found Question 28 difficult because if they answered "yes" they would be without a country—they'd be giving up citizenship in Japan, yet they'd still be denied citizenship in the United States.

Families were torn apart by the loyalty questions. If parents answered "no-no" and children "yes-yes," they might be separated. Some Nisei were ordered by their parents to answer "no-no"; others answered "yes-yes," but chose to go to Tule Lake with their families anyway. Miss Yamauchi went to Tule Lake in order to stay with her relatives. Children like Richard, Makoto, Raymond, Kaoru, George, and Shizuko simply had to follow their mothers and fathers.

Topaz had a high percentage of "no-nos" in comparison to the other camps, because the administrators did not do a good job explaining the questions. Therefore, the internees were confused and suspicious. In the end, 1,447 Nikkei elected to go to Tule Lake and were joined by 95 high-school and 37 elementary-school students. More Nisei (1,062) went than Issei (385), which suggests these American citizens were angry that their constitutional rights were being denied.

Tule Lake Segregation Center was filled with unhappy people, some of whom began to fight back. A few of the internees renounced their American citizenship and openly supported Japan. Other internees at Tule Lake were threatened, even harmed, if they didn't join the militants in their crusade. At their request, a number of Nikkei actually were sent to Japan.

August 12, 1943

Last night there was heavy rain, thunder and lightning.
All the Brownies had lots and lots of fun yesterday at Antelope Springs.

Johnny had a happy surprise yesterday. His mother came home from Provo where she was picking beans. She had been away for almost one month and a half.

Tomorrow, August 13th, is the last day of school. We shall have a "last day of school" party.

This is the last page of our daily diary. We hope everyone has enjoyed it. It has been lots of fun for us.

Good-bye and good luck.

August 12, 1943.

Last night there was heavy rain, thunder and lightning.

All the Brownies had lots and lots of fun yesterday at Antelope Springs.

Johnny had a happy surprise yesterday. His mother came home from Provo where she was picking beans. She had been away for almost one month and a half.

Tomorrow, August 13th is the last day of school. We shall have a "last day of school" party.

This is the last page of our daily diary. We hope everyone has enjoyed it. It has been lots of fun for us.

Good-bye and good luck.

Antelope Springs was ninety miles from Topaz at the foot of Swasey Peak. It was once the site of a Civilian Conservation Corps camp during the Depression years. The CCC was a program to combat unemployment, and as many as 500,000 unmarried young men joined and lived in these camps. They worked on conservation projects, such as flood control and the protection of forests and wildlife. The CCC was disbanded in 1942, and the old campsite near Delta was converted into a recreation area for the residents of Topaz. Also, two buildings were moved from Antelope Springs to Topaz to be used as Christian and Buddhist churches.

Not only the Brownies and Boy Scouts enjoyed camping, swimming, and hiking at Antelope Springs, but also other internees would get passes to roam freely around the 19,000 acres of the project. Trucks transported campers to Antelope Springs and dropped them there. Occasionally someone got lost, but no one ever tried to run away. It seems strange that Topaz was ringed by guard towers and James Wakasa was shot for getting too near a fence, yet the Nikkei could wander an entire mountainside without supervision.

"Tomorrow . . . is the last day of school." Miss Yamauchi and her children finish their diary, realizing that they will not be together at Mountain View School again. Miss Yamauchi and six of the children will be leaving for Tule Lake. Other classmates will resettle or have already resettled in places outside the camp with their parents. By the end of the war, only half of the population of Topaz remained.

Anne Yamauchi Hori and her third graders said "good-bye" and bid their readers "good luck." They understood the need for luck, for theirs had not been good. So, good luck in Tule Lake, they seemed to be saying. Good luck in Idaho or Salt Lake City or in Topaz. Good luck when the war ended, and it was time to go home.

Miss Yamauchi's class of third-grade students at Mountain View School in Topaz. This was the only year in her life that Miss Yamauchi taught school. Edwin Narahara, whose name appears frequently in the diary, is the boy at the top right. Today, Edwin is a successful architect in Los Angeles. *Saburo Hori*

Lillian "Anne" Yamauchi Hori as her third-grade students would remember her. She was one of many unsung heroes who brightened the lives of thousands of relocated children. Mrs. Hori died in 1993.

AFTERWORD

President Roosevelt announced the end of relocation in December of 1944. As of January 1, 1945, the West Coast was no longer off-limits to Japanese Americans. But by the end of January 1945, there were still nearly six thousand people in Topaz. The administration then called them "guests of the government." The relocation centers were to be kept open only long enough "to help the residents make a satisfactory transition to normal life." But for these people, many of whom had lost most of what they owned except their dignity, a normal life was not within easy reach.

The official closing date for Topaz was October 31, 1945, and the government worked furiously to push residents out of the camp. Most of the younger Nisei resettled quickly, leaving Topaz mostly with Issei, many of whom were too old, poor, or frightened to return home. "Here there is little freedom, but we are not stared at," said one such resident. "We don't get what we want here, but we live anyway and do not feel lonely."

Two young men are given a cheery sendoff, along with the others who resettled outside of Topaz or who eventually began to take the journey home.

Some of the Nikkei were so angry that they refused to leave. They considered the resettlement grants of twenty-five dollars (fifty dollars for a family) plus train fare an insult. Let the government who ruined their lives be forced to support them indefinitely. But the U.S. government refused to accept that responsibility. By the deadline, every soul would be squeezed out of Topaz, whether they had a place to go or not.

As the population dwindled, Topaz began to resemble a ghost town. Bit by bit parts of the camp shut down. The schools were closed, never to reopen, in June of 1945. By the end of September, fewer than two thousand people remained. In early November, the camp was empty.

Returning home was painful for many of the internees from Topaz and the other relocation centers. They faced housing and job shortages. Their stored belongings often were either missing or vandalized. Some families were barely able to survive. Edwin Narahara, who remembered his childhood in Topaz as an extended camp-out, also remembered being hungry for the first time when his family returned to California. Ted Nagata's family stayed in Utah, settling in Salt Lake City. But they were so poverty-stricken that Ted's father was forced to leave his children in a Catholic orphanage for a year.

Nikkei also feared discrimination and hostility, and sometimes their fears were justified. Daniel Inouye, a captain in the 442nd Regimental Combat Team and later a U.S. senator from Hawaii, remembers the prejudice he encountered in California when he returned after the war. Though he was in his uniform with its decorations for bravery, a barber refused to cut his hair. "We don't cut Jap hair," he declared.

Saburo Hori stands at the Topaz historical site in May 1995, his first trip back to the camp in over 50 years. The cement slab was the floor of a mess hall.
M. O. Tunnell

The country was slow in acknowledging the wrongs of Japanese-American relocation. In the 1940s and 1950s, the government accepted claims for damage or loss of property from the Nikkei, but the average payment to each internee was only $440. The total amount the government paid to Japanese Americans at that time was about $100 million. In 1983, the congressional Commission on Wartime Relocation and Internment of Civilians (CWRIC) estimated the losses of income and property "for which no compensation was made after the war" to be about $370 million. In 1983 dollars, that would have been as much as $2 billion.

In 1983, the CWRIC recommended to Congress that it pass a resolution apologizing for the wrongs of relocation and that it work to right some of the injustices, such as reversing the less-than-honorable discharges given to many Japanese-American soldiers following Pearl Harbor. The CWRIC also recommended that Congress fund a special foundation to "sponsor research and public education activities" about Japanese-American relocation and similar injustices. And, as a token of apology and to make up in a small degree for losses, the commission recommended a onetime compensation of $20,000 to each survivor.

Finally, Congress passed the Civil Rights Act of 1988, which made the recommendations of the CWRIC into law. Of course, not everyone agreed that there had been a wrong that needed to be righted. Some people who played important roles in the relocation defended their actions. But in October of 1990, the first letters of apology, signed by President George Bush, along with the redress payments, were mailed. For many, the apology came too late.

Fifty years later, survivors of Topaz and their friends gather to dedicate a section of a restored recreation barrack at the Topaz Museum in Delta, Utah.

ACKNOWLEDGMENTS

We wish to thank Susan Whetstone of the Utah State Historical Society for allowing us to photograph Miss Yamauchi's class diary and for helping us locate most of the archival photographs used in this book. Many, many thanks to Saburo Hori and his family, who graciously provided the photographs of his wife and their mother, Lillian "Anne" Yamauchi Hori, and who read our manuscript to check for historical accuracy. We are also grateful to Takako Tsuchiya Endo, Anne's best friend, and Jane Beckwith for reading the manuscript and giving us advice. Others who provided information and encouragement include Grace Oshita, Ted Nagata, and, of course, Edwin Narahara.

In 1995, Saburo Hori sees "Our Class Diary" for the first time. He was unaware that his wife, Anne, had kept this diary with her students.

Reference and Reading List
Other Books about the Japanese-American Relocation and Internment

Bosworth, Allan R. *America's Concentration Camps.* New York: W. W. Norton, 1967.

Daniels, Roger. *Concentration Camps, North America: Japanese in the United States and Canada During World War II.* Malabar, Fla.: Robert E. Krieger Publishing, 1981.

———, Sandra C. Taylor, and Harry H. L. Kitano, eds. *Japanese Americans: From Relocation to Redress.* Rev. ed. Seattle: University of Washington Press, 1991.

*Davis, Daniel S. *Behind Barbed Wire: The Imprisonment of Japanese Americans During World War II.* New York: Dutton, 1982.

*Garrigue, Sheila. *The Eternal Spring of Mr. Ito.* New York: Bradbury, 1985.

*Hamanaka, Sheila. *The Journey: Japanese Americans, Racism, and Renewal.* New York: Orchard, 1990.

James, Thomas. *Exile Within: The Schooling of Japanese Americans 1942–1945.* Cambridge, Mass.: Harvard University Press, 1987.

*Levine, Ellen. *A Fence Away from Freedom: Japanese Americans and World War II.* New York: G. P. Putnam's Sons, 1995.

*Means, Florence Crandall. *The Moved-Outers.* Boston: Houghton Mifflin, 1945.

*Mochizuki, Ken. *Baseball Saved Us.* New York: Lee and Low, 1993.

Okubo, Miné. *Citizen 13660.* Seattle: University of Washington Press, 1983 (1946).

*Stanley, Jerry. *I Am an American.* New York: Crown, 1994.

Taylor, Sandra. *Jewel of the Desert: Japanese American Internment at Topaz.* Berkeley, Calif.: University of California Press, 1993.

Uchida, Yoshiko. *Desert Exile.* Seattle: University of Washington Press, 1982.

*———. *The Invisible Thread.* New York: Julian Messner, 1991.

*———. *Journey Home.* New York: Atheneum, 1978.

*———. *Journey to Topaz.* Berkeley, Calif.: Creative Arts, 1985 (New York: Scribner's, 1971).

*For young readers.

INDEX

Page numbers in italic type refer to illustrations.